This book belongs to

Froggy Day
An original concept by author Heather Pindar
© Heather Pindar
Illustrated by Barbara Bakos

MAVERICK ARTS PUBLISHING LTD
Studio 3A, City Business Centre, 6 Brighton Road, Horsham,
West Sussex, RH13 5BB, +44 (0)1403 256941
© Maverick Arts Publishing Limited
Published September 2018

A CIP catalogue record for this book
is available at the British Library.

ISBN 978-1-84886-321-7

www.maverickbooks.co.uk

Maverick publishing

FROGGY DAY

By Heather Pindar

&

Barbara Bakos

"Watch out!" said the woman on the TV,
"Today is going to be froggy…

…very froggy!"

PLIP-PLOP! PLIP-PLOP! **DOWN** poured the **big, fat** frogs.

The car windows soon got all **frogged** up.
Everyone had to switch on their **defroggers**.

BEEEEEEP!

Use your frog lamps too please, madam.

The traffic jams stretched back for miles.
It made the drivers **hopping** mad.

It was much too **Froggy** on the bus.
The frogs rang the bell. DING! DING-A-LING!

DING!

And **again**! DING! DING-A-LING! And **again**. DING! DING-A-LING!

DING!

Everyone sighed and said, "I can't believe how **froggy** it is today."

"Woof!" said the dogs, "It's too froggy! We don't

want frogs in the park. Shoo, frogs, shoo!"

It was **froggy** in the shops too.

"Call for help,"
said Till Number 5,
"**Frog** in bagging area."

"We could do without all this **Frogginess**," said the builders.

It was **froggy** in the **mixer**...

…and the **digger**.

It even got **froggy** in Jan's **big** **mug** of **tea**.

It was so **froggy** on the farm

that the animals **stampeded**.

The sailors heard the frog warnings on the radio.
All across the bay the **frog horns** boomed eerily.

At the fair it was so **froggy** you could only just squeeze onto the **waltzers**...

...and it was even **froggier** on the **dodgems**.

Then it got **Froggy** at school. Much too **Froggy**.

"We can't have frogs in school!" said Mrs Pickle.

'It's NOT too **froggy** for us!" said the children. "**Hop, hop, hurray**!"

Ribbit! Ribbit! Ribbit!

"It's been the **Froggiest** day since records began,"
said the woman on the TV.

"But you'll need to watch your step tomorrow too…

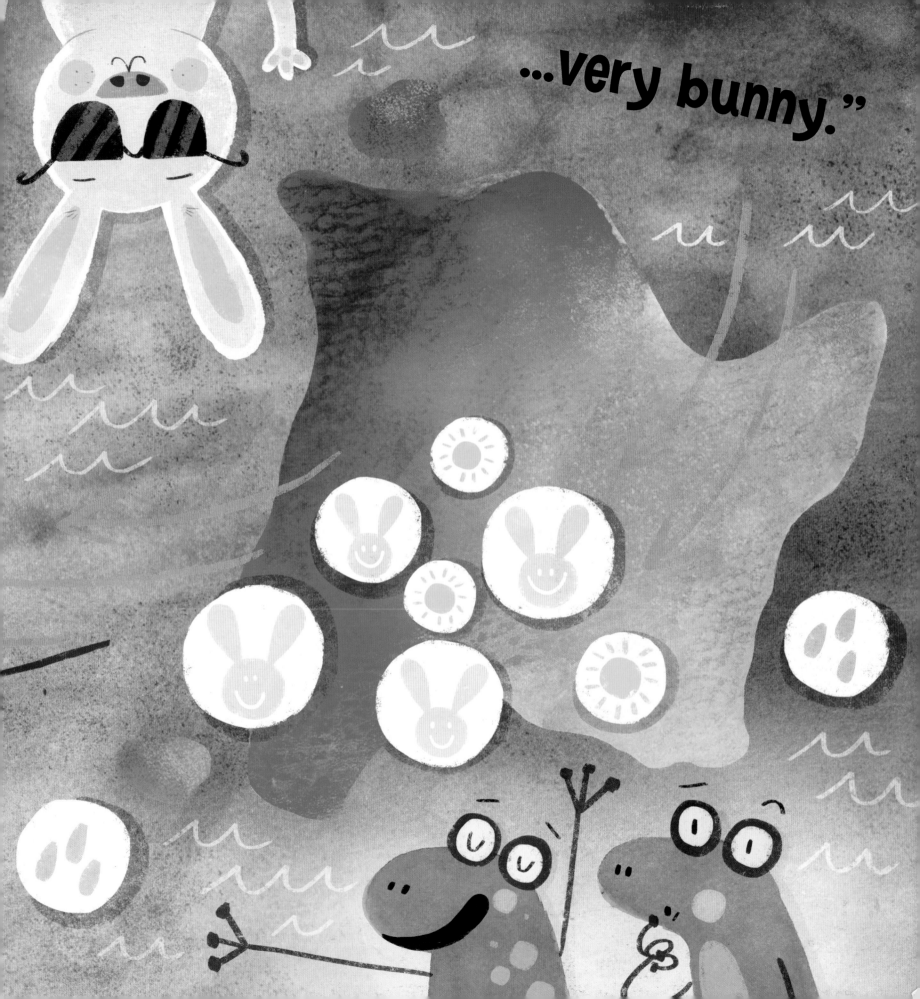

Keep it cool!